IN THE ORCHE

Written and Illustrated

Priyanga Soundar

Ukiyoto Publishing

All global publishing rights are held by
Ukiyoto Publishing
Published in 2022

Content Copyright © Priyanga Soundar

ISBN 9789360162887

All rights reserved.
No part of this publication may be reproduced, transmitted, or stored in a retrieval system, in any form by any means, electronic, mechanical, photocopying, recording, or otherwise, without the prior permission of the publisher.

The moral rights of the author have been asserted.
This is a work of fiction. Names, characters, businesses, places, events, locales, and incidents are either the products of the author's imagination or used in a fictitious manner. Any resemblance to actual persons, living or dead, or actual events is purely coincidental.

This book is sold subject to the condition that it shall not by way of trade or otherwise, be lent, resold, hired out, or otherwise circulated, without the publisher's prior consent, in any form of binding or cover other than that in which it is published.

This title is produced in Association with Pachyderm Tales

www.pachydermtales.com

Dedicated to my parents
Vimalarani & Soundararajan.
My in - laws
Jayanthi & Sambathkumar.
My Nephew **Dhananth,**
My husband **Naresh,**
and My son **Yojith.**
Who are pillars of my strength,
my happiness, and everything!

ACKNOWLEDGMENT

Thank you Geeta Ramanujam and Shantanu Bhasin for funding this book which is a part of the body positivity project.
#Hugyourself

I also whole heartedly thank
Ms. Uma Maheshwari
Ms. Nirmala
Ms. Uma Venkat
Ms. Jayabalasundari
Ms. Rathna Pandian
Ms. Chrishanti Vijay
Ms. Usha Shankaranarayanan
Ms. Sarika
Ms. Sowmya
Ms. Saratha Srinivasan
Ms. Raji
Ms. Christy Elena
Ms. Lakshmi Desigan
Ms. Ravichokkalingam
Ms. Divya Sriharan

This book was a part of workshop conducted in my college,
NGM College, Pollachi and Pachyderm Tales.
I whole heartedly thank all my teachers and HOD of English Dept, NGM as well as Suja Mam for this initiative.

'Garden Orche' a lovely garden was jam-packed with vibrant flowers, fruits, and vegetables.

'Spark' the little fairy was created by God to take care of all the trees, plants, shrubs, and creepers in the garden.

Every day, Spark used to go all around the garden and chitchat with all the members of the garden in a friendly manner.

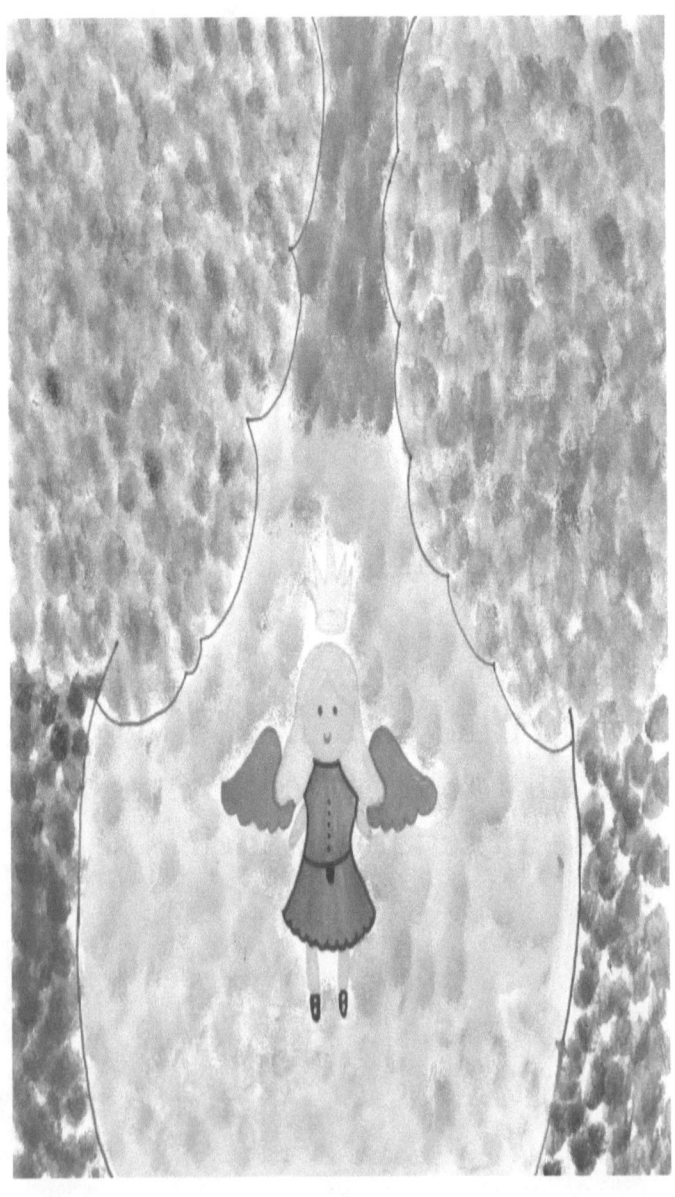

One day,

Spark saw, a few fruits discussing something and apple was addressing them seriously!

As the conversation among fruits went on for a few hours, Spark felt that there might be some problem amidst the fruits.

The little fairy did not want anyone in the garden to indulge in a quarrel or fight. She preferred the garden to be quiet and peaceful.

Spark stood behind the tree, where Apple, Banana, Grapes, Orange, Mango, Pomegranate, Pineapple, Jackfruit, Strawberry, Papaya, and Watermelon had this crucial discussion.

Spark listened to the following conversation:

Apple spoke to all the fruits,

"My dear friends, I am the king of all the fruits. You all must listen to my words and follow my instructions. People love me a lot due to my shape, colour, and flavour. I am in a proper round shape with bright red colour. And I taste sweet which is liked by all. So, I am the king of fruits."

Spark noticed the dramatic effect created by *Apple* to convince the fruits…

As many did not agree with the words of Apple.

Clever and foxy, Apple started **Body Shaming** all the fruits by their shape, discriminating by their colour and it even started blaming the fruits based on its taste.

Apple said to *Orange*,

"Hey Orange, though you are perfectly round shaped like me!

You taste sour and
your complexion is not bright as mine.

Your skin is also rough…

So, you will not be loved by many."

Now Apple spoke to
Banana,

"You poor Banana! You appear extremely thin and curved, your complexion is also pale and you taste sweet but not as sweet as me.

So, you are also not qualified to be the king of fruits."

Apple called out, *Teeny-weeny Grape!*

"You are too little and as a bunch you are overcrowded.

It's impossible for you to stand alone!

You will have a problem with decision-making.

At times, you taste sour as well, so you can never imagine to be the king."

Apple spoke to
Pomegranate:

"Pome! you look a little like me, but it's quite tough to peel you!

and your juice can stain, which annoys people.

So, you don't have a chance as a King!"

Apple stated, "*Oh Lovely Strawberry*,

Your complexion is better than mine but your improper shape... Your skin... with its rough texture, and sweaty sour taste definitely brings your position down!"

Apple shouted,

"Oh! Thorns! Thorns! Thorns!

My *dear Pineapple* and *Jackfruit*,

"Please remember, your look spoils everything!

People hate you blindly as you both are tough to handle.

Soften yourself please!"

Apple said,

"*Mango* can you please explain to me about your shape?

I find it difficult to classify your shape.

You keep on changing your colour and you taste sour during early stages and terribly sour in later stages.

So, you can never wish to be the king."

Apple told *Papaya*,

"Your complexion is not at all attractive. Let's not even talk about your taste. Yuck!

Your shape is different and you have a lot of seeds.

It's tough for people to handle as you are too slippery.

So, no one loves you!"

Apple shouted,

"Ahhh! *Giant Watermelon*!

Uff! It's too tough to lift you. You are properly oversized!

You are too juicy and you have a lot of seeds which disturbs people while eating.
There is too much wastage while eating you.
And you taste bland.

So, you cannot even imagine being the king of fruits!"

28   Priyanga Soundar

Apple declared,

"So finally my dear friends! I am the one and only fruit loved by all and I must be **The King!**"

At this point, Spark interrupted and started addressing all the fruits.

Spark asked, "Hello my dear lovely fruits. I hope you all are doing well. May I join this serious conversation?"

Apple replied with a smirk,

"I have been waiting for a moment like this! Please join us!

We are talking about how I am eligible to be the king of fruits and you came at the right time!"

Spark questioned,

"King of fruits? Who? How were you selected?"

All the fruits except Apple had sad faces and complained.

"Apple has been telling us that he is The king of all fruits. Because he is properly round shaped. He has a Bright red complexion and he is sweetest when it comes to taste.
And because of these people love him!
And since we lack these qualities. People love him more than us!"

Spark said,

"My dear smart Apple! I am happy that you convinced your friends using your clever words. I am proud of you!

But you too have defects… like your friends."

Apple enquired angrily,

"Defect?

What is the defect that you see in me?

I am perfect every way!"

Spark replied softly,

"Listen my dear lovely Apple, you are in a round shape but not as round as orange!"

"Pretty Apple! you also have shades of red, green, and yellow.

You do not appear bright red always."

"Adorable Apple! you are a little sweet and a little tart.

At times Mangoes, Oranges, Bananas, Jackfruits, Grapes, Strawberries, and Watermelons are sweeter than you!"

"Cute little Apple! The texture of Mango, Grapes, Pomegranate, Watermelon and Banana are far better than yours."

After listening to the words of Spark,

Apple was in the verge of tears!

Spark now consoled Apple,

"Everyone of us is best in our own way!

We all have our positives and negatives.

No one is superior to the other.

We always have to talk good about others!"

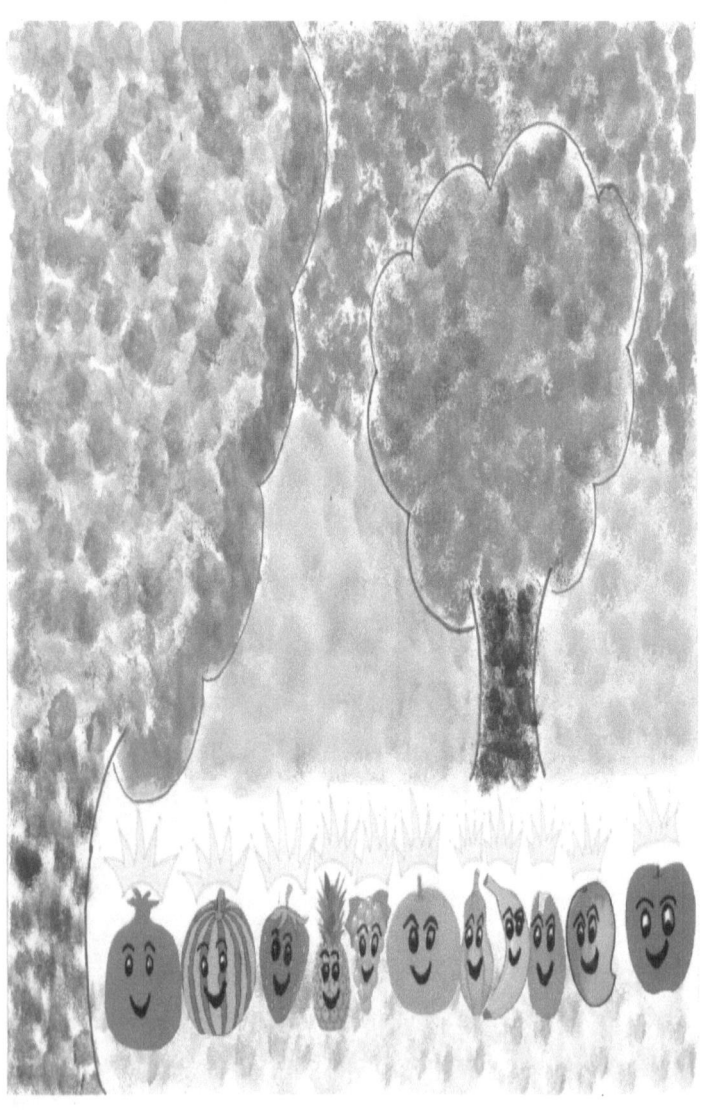

Spark said,

"All fruits contain various vitamins and minerals which are essential for the human body!

Rich nutrients help to lead a healthy life.

People live a healthy life when all of you are mixed in a proper proposition."

From then on, all the fruits accepted the words of Fairy Spark and lived happily in the orche.

The Author

Priyanga Soundar is currently pursuing her Doctoral research degree in English Literature. She was brought up listening to stories of fairies narrated by her mother who was working as a teacher. In her childhood, she used to visualise green grapes with twinkling eyes, singing songs, waving hands, and dancing legs, which was the inspiration for her to write this story! She also narrates bedtime stories to her 3-year-old son, where she combines moral values with teaching about shapes, colours, fruits, vegetables, vehicles, and many more.

www.ingramcontent.com/pod-product-compliance
Lightning Source LLC
LaVergne TN
LVHW041554070526
838199LV00046B/1962